The MAGIC Bedtime Storybook

Vivian French

Illustrated by Emily Bolam

Orion
Children's Books

For Lucy, Amy, Eleanor and Matilda.
Thanks for the use of your kitchen to write in!
Love, Viv xxx

First published in Great Britain in 2005
by Orion Children's Books
a division of the Orion Publishing Group Ltd
Orion House
5 Upper St Martin's Lane
London WC2H 9EA

Text copyright © Vivian French 2005
Illustrations copyright © Emily Bolam 2005

Designed by Tracey Cunnell

A catalogue record for this book is available from the British Library

Printed in Italy by Printer Trento
ISBN 1 84255 168 X

CONTENTS

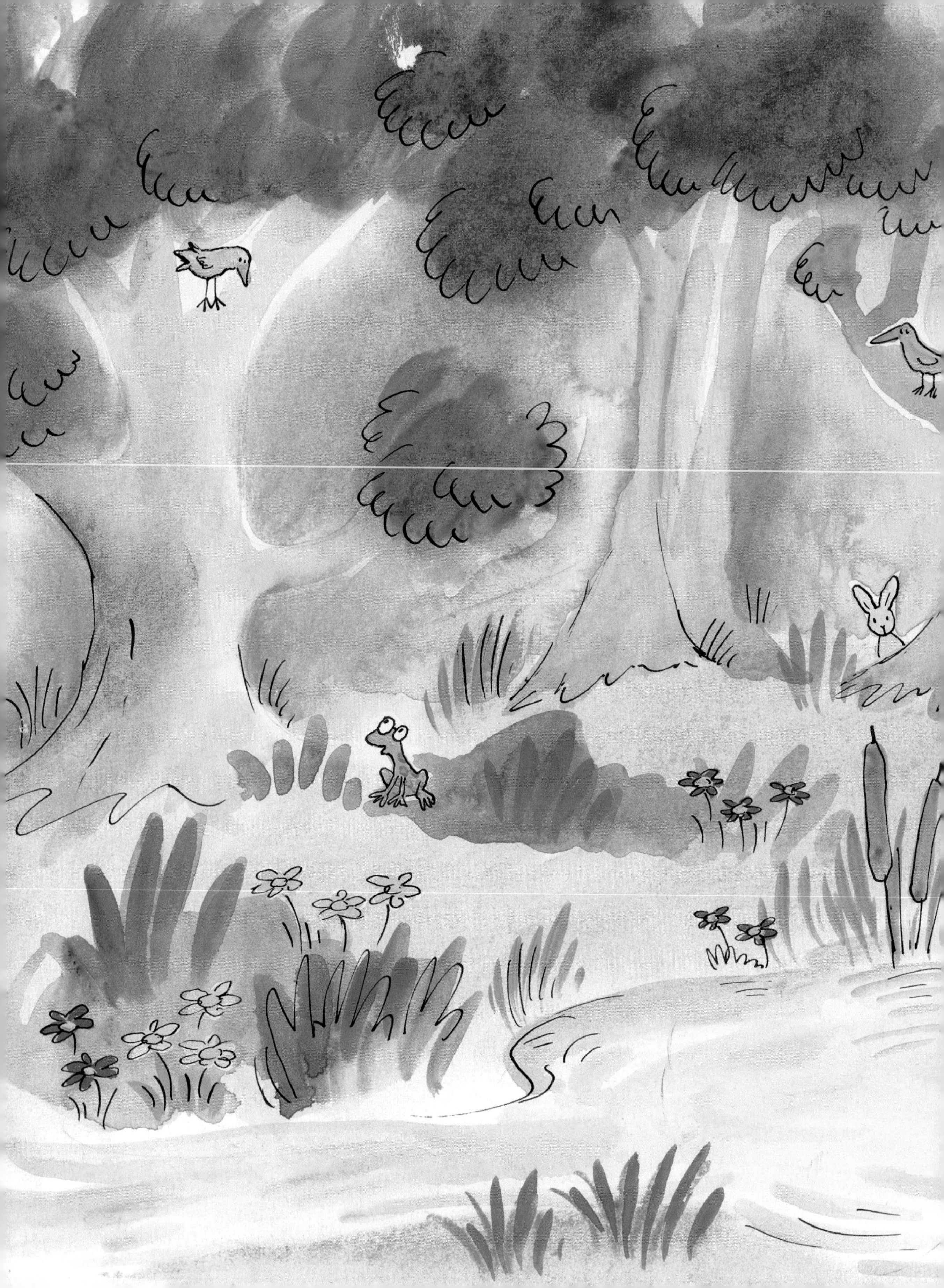

The Beginning

Long long ago there was
a forest of tall green trees . . .
and on the edge of the forest was a pond . . .
and in the pond lived a family of frogs.
Spotty Frog was the smallest of all the frog family.
He was so small that he often got forgotten,
but he didn't mind. He'd hop out of the pond,
and go exploring, and his mother never noticed.
Most of the time this didn't matter,
but one day Spotty's mum had something
very important to say. She sat all Spotty's
many brothers and sisters down
and told them a secret.

She told them the forest was a MAGIC forest, and she made them promise that they would never ever talk about it except in whispers . . . but Spotty didn't hear a word she said. Spotty was out under the trees, and Spotty had discovered singing.

"Mum! MUM!" he shouted, "LISTEN TO ME!" He hopped onto a stone, and began to sing, and although he was a very little frog he had a LOUD voice. He sang,

"Oh, have you seen the fairies oh, the fairies oh, the fairies oh.

Oh have you seen the fairies oh, as they go dancing by?"

At once there was a huge commotion all around him. Birds squawked, squirrels chattered, rabbits stamped their feet as loudly as they could – and Spotty Frog's mother leapt out of the pond.

"SHHH!" she said. "SH, Spotty Frog! You mustn't sing songs like that!" She looked anxiously all around. "You might be heard! HUMAN BEINGS come into our forest, and if they hear you singing a song like that – OH DEARIE DEARIE ME! We'd never get rid of them ever again!"

"Why not, Mum?" asked Spotty, his eyes very round.

"Because – " and Mrs Frog whispered as quietly as she could. "No boys and girls must ever know that our forest is a MAGIC forest. If they did, they'd chase Dragon Silverclaw, and upset Big Giant Busybones – and do all kinds of terrible things!"

"Oh," said Spotty. "I see."

"So you must promise me your best ever promise," said Mrs Frog. "You must promise me you'll never ever tell anyone EVER that this is a magic forest."

Spotty nodded. "I promise," he said.

"That's all right then," Mrs Frog said with a huge sigh. "You were SO lucky that no little boys and girls were near. They're terribly, terribly dangerous. Now, let's forget it ever happened." And she hopped back into the pond with a PLOP!

Around the pond the birds went back to singing, the squirrels went off to hunt for nuts, and the rabbits scampered away. Spotty Frog sighed, and tried hard to think of another song to sing.

"FROGGY!"

Spotty jumped, and looked round.

"Hey! Froggy! I'm over here!"

Spotty stared. A huge clump of reeds was rustling and shaking. Spotty's eyes grew rounder and rounder as a head popped out.

"Hello, Froggy!" said the head. "I'm Ruby. What's your name?"

Spotty didn't answer. He was too surprised.

Ruby pushed her way out of the reeds. "You must have a name," she said, and she shoved Spotty off his stone and sat down on it herself.

Spotty swallowed hard. "Are you . . . " he swallowed again. "Are you . . . a GIRL?"

Ruby put her head on one side. "I might be," she said.

Spotty gulped. "If you're a girl I can't talk to you," he whispered, and he was just about to dive into the water when Ruby grabbed his arm.

"Just a minute, SPOTTY!" she said, and she didn't sound very friendly. "Don't you go running away! I was listening to your song and, what's more, I heard every single word your mum said to you . . . so you'd better do what I say! Because if you don't, " and Ruby gave Spotty's arm a pinch, "I'm going to tell every human being I can find all about you and your fairies and giants and dragons and witches – " Ruby suddenly stopped.

If Spotty had been watching Ruby's face
he would have seen that she had blushed very pink,
but he was much too frightened to do anything except
tremble.

"Oh no," he whimpered. "Please don't say you're a girl!
Please don't go chasing Big Giant Busybones! My mum's a nice
mum, but she does get VERY cross . . . "

"We'll do a deal," Ruby said. "You help me find something I've lost in
the forest, and I promise I won't tell."

Spotty nodded. "I'll help you. I know every single path in the wood!"

"Good," said Ruby. "Come on then – let's start now!"

"NOW?" said Spotty. "Now this very minute?"

Ruby folded her arms. "We made a bargain, frog. If you want
me to keep quiet . . . "

Spotty leapt up. "I'm ready!" he said. "We'll start at once!
What have you lost?"

Big Giant Busybones was sitting outside his house
watching the world go by. He smiled when he saw Spotty.
"Hello, Spotty Frog!" he boomed. "And how are you today?
Have you brought someone new to meet me?"
Spotty waved an arm. "This is Ruby," he said.
"She's collecting stories."
"Is she indeed?" Big Giant Busybones nodded.

"Sit yourselves down, and I'll tell you the story of Big Billy's birthday."

Big Billy

told by Big Giant Busybones

Once there was a giant called Big Billy, who lived in a magic wood. Every year the fairy queen made him a cake for his birthday, but he always ended the day eating bread and jam because he was still hungry.

"The trouble is that nobody eats as much as I do," Big Billy said mournfully. "Fairy cake is very tasty, but it's gone in a mouthful! If there was another giant in this wood he'd understand. He'd make me a great BIG cake . . . " Then Big Billy suddenly smiled.

"I know!" he said. "I'LL make a cake! Why didn't I think of that before?" He looked at his calendar. "Three days until my birthday! Now, how do you make a cake? Maybe I'll ask the trolls."

Big Billy went stomping down the path to the trolls' house. Mottle, Lollibob and Dada Tock were trying to balance on each other's shoulders, and were wet and dirty from falling into the mud. When they saw Big Billy coming they cheered loudly.

"Please, Mr Giant," they said, "our kite is stuck in that tree! Can you fetch it down for us?"

"Of course," said Big Billy. He stretched out his arm and picked the kite out of the branches, but it took him a long time to untangle the string.

"THANK YOU!" said the trolls when the kite was safe at last. "How lucky you were going by!"

"Actually," Big Billy said, "I'm making a cake for my birthday party. Everyone's invited – but I don't know what cakes are made of."

"Water and mud," said Lollibob.

"Snails and worms," said Mottle.

"Beetles and bugs," said Dada Tock.

"Oh," said Big Billy, "are you sure?"

The trolls all nodded, and Big Billy stomped away from the trolls muttering "waterandmudandsnailsandwormsandbeetles and bugs" to himself – but he was so tired that instead of going to the shop he went home and went to bed.

The next morning Big Billy woke up with a start.

"Oh NO!" he said worriedly. "What on earth do I DO with the waterandmudandsnailsandwormsandbeetles and bugs when I've got them? I'd better ask the pixies."

So Big Billy went stomping along the path to the pixies' house. He found them sitting on the banks of the stream.

"Hello, Big Billy!" they said. "Can you help? Our tree trunk bridge has been washed away, and we can't get across to pick blackberries."

"I'll fetch it back for you," said Big Billy, and he waded into the water. It took him a long time to drag the tree trunk back, but it was safely in place at last.

"Now," said Big Billy, "I'm making a cake for my birthday party, and everyone's invited – but what on earth do I DO with the waterandmudandsnailsandwormsandbeetles and bugs?"

"Water and mud and snails?" said Seed.

"Worms and beetles and bugs?" said Sparkle.

"YUCK!" said Wink. "That's a TROLL cake. You need acorns and oakapples!"

"And dandelions and daisies," said Sparkle.

"And a cupful of sunshine," said Seed.

"Then mix it all together and cook it," said Wink.

"Oh, THANK YOU!" said Big Billy, and he stomped away.

"Shall I go and get the acornsandoakapplesanddandelionsanddaisies and a cupful of sunshine now?" he wondered. "No. I'm too tired. I'll go shopping tomorrow."

The next morning Big Billy got up early. "It's nearly my birthday!" he said. "I'll do my shopping, and then I'll make my cake." He picked up his basket, and stomped off in between the trees to Old Fairy Glimmerwing's store. When he got there Old Fairy Glimmerwing was trying to rock Baby Peapod to sleep.

"I'm making a cake for my birthday, and everyone's invited!" Big Billy shouted. "And – "

"WAAAAAAA!" yelled Baby Peapod.

"Oh, Mr Giant!" said Old Fairy Glimmerwing. "PLEASE could you rock the baby? I'm worn to a shadow!"

So Big Billy rocked Baby Peapod. He sang her a little lullaby. He hushed her and he soothed her. He rocked her again, and at last she went to sleep.

"Thank you SO much," said Old Fairy Glimmerwing. "And what was it you wanted?"

Big Billy scratched his head. Was it acorns and worms? Was it sunshine and mud? Was it dandelions and beetles?

"I can't remember," Big Billy said, "I'll have to come back again later."

Off he stomped, but when he got home he flopped into his favourite armchair.

"I'll just have a little snooze," he said . . .

and he slept . . . and he slept . . . and he slept . . . and he slept . . .

z Z Z Z

and he didn't wake up until Giddle the goblin tweaked his ear and said,

"HAPPY BIRTHDAY, BIG BILLY!"

Big Billy sat up and rubbed his eyes. His house was FULL of pixies and trolls and fairies, and witches and dwarves and a dragon, and a wizard and a wise old owl.

"Oh NO!" he groaned. "Oh NO! You're here for my birthday, and I haven't made the . . . "

Big Billy stopped, and sniffed. Then he sniffed again . . . and when he looked at his table he saw a great big beautiful giant-sized birthday cake.

"We mixed it!" said Lollibob.

"And we stirred it!" said Sparkle.

"You helped us so we came
to help you," said Seed.

"But you were asleep," said Mottle.

"And snoring!" said Dada Tock.

"So we just got on with it," said Wink.

"With a BIG pinch of magic," smiled Old Fairy Glimmerwing.

"Thank you very VERY much," said Big Billy.

And as he blew out his candles everyone sang "Happy Birthday to YOU!"

And it was the best birthday cake ever . . . except for just one thing.

There were so many people at Big Billy's party that he was only able to have one large slice . . . and he ended the day eating bread and jam because he was still hungry.

"Next year I'll make TWO cakes," he said sleepily. "One for my party, and one for me!"

"I do like stories about cake," said Spotty, "thank you very much!"

Ruby fixed Big Giant Busybones with a hard gaze. "Was it about you? Are you Big Billy?"

Big Giant Busybones laughed so much that the tiles on his roof rattled.

"Ho ho ho!" he chortled. "Yes – it was me! You're a clever little thing to guess! And the next time I have a birthday, you two must come to my party. Here – wait just a minute!" And Big Giant Busybones stomped off into his house. He came back holding a little wooden spoon.

"Here's something to help you remember my story," he said. "And it'll remind you to come to my party!"

28

Ruby put the spoon in her bag, and grabbed Spotty's hand. "Come on, Spotty. Where are we going next?"

Spotty looked at her in horror. "Aren't you going to say 'Thank You'?" he asked.

"Thanks, Big Billy," Ruby said as she marched Spotty away. "Now, get walking, frog!"

Spotty didn't say anything. He thought Ruby was one of the rudest creatures he had ever met. On the other hand, Spotty loved stories better than anything else in the world . . .

"Maybe I won't run away just yet," he thought. "Maybe I'll see what Wise Old Owl thinks of her. He knows everything about everything." And he hopped in and out of the trees with Ruby following close behind him.

Wise Old Owl lived high up
in the branches of a beech tree.
"However can we get up there?" Ruby asked as
Spotty pointed out the neat little house tucked cosily in
against the tree trunk. "I haven't got my broom – "
She suddenly turned purple, and began to cough.
Spotty didn't notice. He was looking for the stone that
Wise Old Owl always left tucked under a bramble bush,
and as soon as he found it he tapped the tree trunk
seven times. There was a rustling from up above,
and a sleepy voice called out, "Who's there?"
"It's me, Spotty Frog!" Spotty shouted.
"I'm sorry to bother you, Wise Old Owl,
but please could you tell me and my . . .
and Ruby a story?"
There was a pause.

"Couldn't you come back tonight?"
Wise Old Owl asked at last. "It's a full moon,
and I'll be much more awake then . . ."
Ruby clutched at Spotty's arm so hard it hurt.
"It's a full moon TONIGHT? Oh NO! I've just GOT
to get my story bag full by then . . . make him tell us a story!
Make him, or I'll tell the boys and girls about You Know What!"
Spotty's heart began to race. "PLEASE, Wise old Owl!"
he pleaded. "PLEASE! We'll be EVER so grateful!"
There was a flapping, and a fluttering,
and a ruffled owl appeared.
'H'mph," he said. "I'll tell you a story about
a bossy little owl called Morton. And then
I'm going straight back to bed!"

Morton the Owl

told by Wise Old Owl

Morton was the last owl to hatch. His brother and sister looked at him in amazement.

"Goodness!" said Eric. "We thought you were a rotten egg!"

"But it's very nice to see you," said Maud.

Morton waved a claw. "Of course it is," he said. "I may be last, but you'll find that I am a very important owl, and you two are very lucky to have me as a brother."

"Oh," said Eric.

"Oh," said Maud.

"And now," Morton said, "I think I can see our mother approaching. And he swept Eric and Maud to one side so he could bow to Mother Owl as she landed.

"Most beautiful of mothers," Morton said, "we meet at last!"

"Hoot HOOT!" said Mother Owl. "What a dear little chick!"

As the days went by Morton grew. Every time Mother Owl came to the nest to feed her babies Morton was always first in line.

"It's not fair!" Eric complained.

"We never get anything nice!" wailed Maud.

"Mother agrees that I am a very important owl," Morton said. He fixed his mother with a hard stare. "Aren't I, Mother dearest?"

Mother Owl looked at him fondly. "Funny little thing," she said.

By the time the owl chicks were ready to leave their nest even Mother Owl was tired of Morton.

"Let's have no more nonsense," she said. "You'll go to school this evening with Eric and Maud, and you'll learn some manners." She waved a claw at him. "Wise Old Owl doesn't hold with little birds getting too big for their boots, you know!"

Morton strode to the edge of the nest. "School may be all very well for foolish little owls like Eric and Maud," he said, "but I know what I know, and that's quite enough for me!" And he spread his wings and jumped . . . and dropped like a stone on top of a group of goblins.

"Excuse me," Morton said as he struggled onto his feet. "A small navigational error."

The goblins picked themselves up and stared at Morton.

"It's a owl!" said Giddle.

"A owl that can't fly," said Slim.

"Tee hee!" said Botch. "He might be VERY useful! Owls can see in the dark – right?"

"Of course," said Morton. "Now, if you'd just help me back to my nest – "

"Oh, no no NO, Mr Owl!" said Botch. "We've got a little job for you! You're JUST what we need!"

Morton fluffed out his feathers. "Really?" he said. "Amazing! Of course I always knew I was a very important owl, but it's good to find that people like yourselves know it too."

"What's he on about?" hissed Slim.

"Don't know," said Giddle.

"Come on, Owl!" ordered Botch. "Get moving – this way!"

"Hey!" said Morton, "I say! Just a minute – " but Botch had him firmly gripped by one wing, and Slim had the other, and they hurried along a dark and twisting path.

At long last the goblins stopped.

"'Ere we are!" whispered Slim. "Look at THAT!"

Morton looked, and saw a big black cave right in front of him. A tiny twist of smoke drifted out into the twilight, and he could hear gentle snoring.

"A very fine cave," he said. "Yes, an excellent cave. But I think I'll be on my way now – "

"Oh no you won't!" said Giddle. "You're going in that cave with us, and you ain't going to make a SOUND!"

"Yeah," said Botch. "'Cos if you do, the dragon'll eat you!"

"DRAGON?" squeaked Morton.

"'Sright," said Slim. "There's a dragon in that cave . . . but there's also lots of GOLD! We're going to creep in and borrow some while he's fast asleep. But WE can't see in the dark, so that's where YOU come in! You trot along in front of us, and show us where it is!"

Morton drew himself up to his full height. "Certainly NOT!" he said. "I'm a very – OUCH!"

Botch waved a tail feather in the air. "Get moving, owl, or you'll be bald as an egg!"

Morton tiptoed into the cave, the goblins close behind him.

"Cor!" Botch muttered, "'S so dark, 's like having a blanket over your head!"

Morton blinked his round yellow eyes . . . and saw a big green eye wink back.

"Eeek!" said Morton.

"Shhh!" Giddle hissed.

The eye winked again, and this time Morton winked back. He saw the dragon smile, and beckon him closer with a steely claw. Morton made himself take seven more steps.

"The gold's just here," he whispered to Giddle. "Bend down, and you'll feel it."

Giddle let go of Morton's wing and grabbed –

and the dragon leapt.

"BOOOO!" he shouted.

There was a mad shrieking as the goblins
scrambled for the entrance. Out they tumbled into
the night as fast as they could go.

Morton bowed politely to the dragon.

"Thank you, dear sir," he said.

"No worries," said the dragon in a sleepy voice. "They're always
trying that trick. Last time it was a mole." He yawned. "Run along,
there's a good fellow. I need my sleep . . . " and he sighed such a long
sigh that Morton was blown out of the cave –

up into the air –

and found himself flying in and out of the trees.

"I can fly!" he yelled, "I can FLY!"

"Excellent," hooted the voice of Wise Old Owl in his ear. "You'll be able to fly
onto that branch, young owl. You're just in time for the first day of school . . . "

"Did he learn to be nicer in school?" Spotty asked.

Wise Old Owl yawned. "Yes," he said. "I think he did."

"I LIKED Morton," Ruby said. "Come on, Frog. We've got to go."

"Hoot! Just one minute, young lady," Wise Old Owl said. He put his head on one side. "Where are YOUR manners?"

"Thankyouverymuchfor the story," Ruby gabbled.

"That's better." Wise Old Owl nodded, and handed her a snow-white feather. "Put this in your story bag. It'll remind you of Morton's story, and it might even remind YOU to say Thank You from time to time. Even little witches need manners, you know. Now, I'm going back to bed . . . " And Wise Old Owl was gone.

Spotty stared after him, puzzled. "What did he mean?" he asked. "What little witches? There aren't any witches here."

"NOTHING," Ruby said. "He didn't mean ANYTHING!" She looked so fierce that Spotty gulped, and made up his mind to go home, whatever Ruby threatened.

"Goodbye, Ruby," he said, hoping that Ruby couldn't see that he was trembling. "Goodbye. Er . . . good luck with your stories!"

Ruby stamped her foot . . . and then stopped. Spotty was already hopping off.

"SPOTTY!" Ruby shouted, but Spotty took no notice. Ruby gulped, and ran after him. "Spotty Frog, don't go! I promise I won't shout at you again . . . but PLEASE can we go and find another story? I really really need to fill my bag!"

Spotty hesitated. Ruby sounded as if she was close to tears, and he was a kind little frog.

"All right," he said at last. "We'll go and see the Giant Oak. He's quite near here."

"THANK YOU," said Ruby, and for the first time she really meant it.

Ruby put her hand in her pocket and pulled out a little velvet bag. "They fell out of here," she said. "I had a whole bag full of them, and I was going to use them for – " Ruby hesitated for a moment. "I was going to use them for something very important that a silly little frog like you doesn't need to know about, and then I found they'd all fallen out and I'd lost them! And I MUST find some more before the moon is full, or – " she hesitated again. "Or I won't get my special something."

Spotty looked at the bag. It didn't look very big. "So what were you collecting?" he asked. "Pebbles? Nuts? Conkers?"

"No," Ruby said. "Stories."

"OH!" Spotty's eyes opened very wide. "I LOVE stories!"

"Good," said Ruby. "So – where are we going first?"

Spotty thought hard. "Ummmm," he said, "maybe we should go and see Big Giant Busybones. He tells wonderful stories."

"Good," said Ruby. "Let's go! Get hopping, Spotty!"

The Giant Oak was humming to
himself as Spotty and Ruby pushed their
way through the buttercups towards him.
"SUCH a lovely day," he said cheerfully, "and it's full
moon tonight!" He lowered his voice to a rumbling whisper.
"And will you two chickens be watching the fairies dancing?"
Ruby gave an odd little gasp, but Spotty smiled.
"If my mum lets me," he said. "But Mr Giant Oak,
would you be very kind and tell me and my friend
a story? Ruby's collecting them, you see."
The Giant Oak rustled his branches happily.

The Giant Oak

"Delighted, my little froggy friend. Always a pleasure to tell a story . . .
now, let me see. Yes! I'll tell you the story of a terrible time
when the ogres came into our wood . . ."

The Ogres

told by the Giant Oak

Once there was a wood, and in the middle of the wood there was an oak tree. Like all oak trees he did his best to look after the little creatures that lived under his shade and up in his branches, and for many years he lived a happy, peaceful life. But then, one dark misty evening, two ogres with long hairy arms and big yellow teeth came trundling into the wood, and they dug themselves a home right under his roots.

"Hey!" said the oak tree, and he wriggled his roots as hard as he could. "You can't live here!" But the ogres took no notice. They hung their washing on the bushes. They stamped on the bluebells and trampled on the celandines. They threw the washing-up water anywhere they pleased, and the ground was littered with their potato peelings and mouldy old tea bags.

The oak tree was very unhappy. Spring was coming, and soon there would be baby squirrels bouncing on his branches. Baby bunnies would be hopping in the grass nearby . . . and down below would be hungry

42

Mr Ogre, and ravenous Mrs Ogre.

One day, the oak tree heard the ogres talking.

"It's time to fetch our big round cooking pot!" said Mrs Ogre.

"Indeed it is!" said Mr Ogre. "And it's time to collect a big pile of sticks!"

"Yum yum!" said Mrs Ogre. "Just think of all those delicious spring suppers! Bunny pie and squirrel stew!" And she rubbed her belly.

"I can't wait!" said Mr Ogre, and he smacked his lips. "I'm SO tired of potatoes and tea."

The oak tree trembled all over. "What shall I do?" he thought. "There must be something I can do."

"You go and get the cooking pot," said Mr Ogre, "and I'll collect the sticks."

"No," said Mrs Ogre. "YOU get the cooking pot, and I'LL collect the sticks."

"NO!" said Mr Ogre. "I'm MUCH better at stick collecting, and you're bigger than me. YOU go and collect the pot."

"It's uphill all the way from our old house," said Mrs Ogre. "I'll get tired."

Mr Ogre looked for a moment as if he might bite Mrs Ogre, but instead he said, "We'll BOTH go and get the pot, and then we'll BOTH collect the sticks."

And they stamped away, still bickering.

The oak tree watched them go, and then, with all his strength, he heaved at his mighty roots . . . but they hardly stirred. He tried again, and this time there was a splintering noise from the ogres' kitchen. The tree smiled grimly, and heaved once more. There was an enormous crash, and the kitchen roof fell in.

The oak tree groaned, and sank back into the earth. He closed his eyes, and he didn't wake until the ogres came back late that night.

Mr and Mrs Ogre were both in a very bad temper from heaving and rolling the big heavy pot up the hill, and when they saw the state of their house they grew even angrier.

"That's YOUR fault!" grumbled Mr Ogre. "I TOLD you we should never have moved!"

"But it was YOU that said we should live under this tree," snapped Mrs Ogre. "And now look! We can't get in through the front door, and it's starting to rain!"

"We can sort it out tomorrow," said Mr Ogre. "Don't make such a fuss!"

"I'll give YOU a fuss in a minute," said Mrs Ogre, and she yawned. "I'm going to go to bed, and as I can't go to bed in my house I'm going to sleep in the pot, and you'd better not wake me up."

"Just a minute!" Mr Ogre's eyebrows were trembling with rage. "Why should it be YOU that sleeps in the pot? I don't want rain dripping on my head all night! I'M going to sleep in the pot!" And he jumped inside. At once Mrs Ogre jumped after him, and they tweaked each other's huge flappy ears, and they pinched each other's big red noses, and they pulled each other's tufty orange hair . . . and the oak tree hauled at his roots one final time.

The big round cooking pot began to roll.

It rolled and it rolled and it rolled, and the ogres inside were twirled round and round until they were giddy as giddy could be, and all they could see were whirling stars.

On and on rolled the pot . . . and it was never ever seen again – and neither were Mr and Mrs Ogre.

"Oooh," said Spotty. "I'm GLAD they went away!"

Ruby jumped to her feet. "Thank you very much indeed," she said before Spotty could say anything.

The Giant Oak beamed at her. "I'm glad you enjoyed it, chicken."

"But now we've got to go," Ruby went on. "Spotty's going to find me another story – aren't you, Spotty?"

"Oh yes." Spotty bent down, and picked up an acorn. "Hey! Here's a reminder for you."

Ruby popped the acorn into her bag. "Where are we going next?" she asked. "Who else tells stories?"

"Try Wizard Gleek," the Giant Oak suggested. "He always has a tale or two to tell. He lives that way!" And he waved a massive branch.

"Good idea!" Ruby said. "Come on, Spotty!" And she pulled Spotty after her as she set off the way the Giant Oak had pointed.

Wizard Gleek's roof was steep and pointed, with sparkly blue
tiles, and a weathervane that spun round and round whether the
wind was blowing or not. When Spotty Frog rang the doorbell
a puff of purple smoke floated out through the keyhole,
and made Spotty and Ruby sneeze.
"Sorry about that," Wizard Gleek said as he opened the door. "I was
trying out a spell for hot buttered toast, but it went wrong . . .
goodness gracious me!" The wizard bent down to peer
at his visitors. "If it isn't a froglet and a – "
"PLEASE could you tell us a story?" Ruby interrupted, and
she waved her bag under the wizard's nose. "I'm collecting
them, and I'm sure you'll tell us a LOVELY one . . . "

"H'm." Wizard Gleek straightened up, and stroked his beard. "I don't
know what you're up to, my dear . . . but I'm sure a story won't hurt.
Come on in!" and he showed Ruby and Spotty inside.
"I'll tell you about my dear old Uncle Bumblespell," the wizard said,
as the three of them sat down on a furry rug painted with
moons and stars. "He was a fine old fellow . . ."

Wizard Bumblespell

told by Wizard Gleek

Wizard Bumblespell was one hundred and ninety-two years old when he lost his wand. He woke up one Saturday morning and went downstairs – and it wasn't on the kitchen table where he always left it.

"Dearie dearie me!" he muttered as he searched under the table and round the wobbly piles of saucepans on the draining board. "Wherever can it be?"

He looked in his workroom, but it wasn't there. There were dusty bottles and spiders, and dried bats and bunches of herbs, and heaps and heaps of books of spells, but no wand.

"Maybe it's slipped underneath something?" Wizard Bumblespell wondered. "Oh dearie dearie DEARIE me. I really must have a tidy up . . . it must be at least a hundred years since the last time. But I HATE tidying . . . oh, if ONLY I could find my wand!" And he went back to have another look in his kitchen. He found several things he didn't know he'd lost, like half a tin of wishing biscuits, two clothes pegs, a sleepy hedgehog, three chewed pencils, a knitting needle and a star catcher, but no wand.

By the next morning Wizard Bumblespell still hadn't found his wand, and he was missing it badly. He couldn't light his fire, because he did it by magic. He couldn't cook his breakfast because he couldn't light his fire, and he couldn't have a nice hot cup of Wizard's Best Brew because he couldn't boil his kettle.

"Oh, misery me!" he said, and he stumped off to see his old friend Witch Willow-water.

Witch Willow-water was sitting in her garden knitting a long and brightly coloured scarf when Wizard Bumblespell came puffing through her gate.

"Good morning, dear friend," she said. "How are you?"

"I've lost my wand," Wizard Bumblespell told her. "I can't find it anywhere, and I don't know what to do!"

Witch Willow-water shook her head. "That's dreadful!" she said. "Come and sit down, and let's see if we can work it out. When did you last use it?"

Wizard Bumblespell thought hard. "I had it on Monday," he said, "because the pixies asked me to put a Bend Down Your Branches spell on their blackberry bushes."

"Good," said Witch Willow-water, and her knitting needles glowed pink and yellow. "What about Tuesday?"

Wizard Bumblespell began to chuckle. "Mottle the troll came running because his Aunt Bulge had got stuck in her doorway! I had to make TWO Set You Free spells, she was so fat!"

"And Wednesday?" Witch Willow-water asked.

"Wednesday . . . now let me see . . . " Wizard Bumblespell tried to remember, but the end of the knitted scarf kept wrapping itself round his legs. "Erm . . . oh, do go AWAY, scarf!"

Witch Willow-water tapped a knitting needle, and the scarf went a grumpy purple and unwound itself.

"I'm so sorry," she said. "It's behaving VERY oddly. Now, you were saying?"

"Nobody came to see me on Wednesday," Wizard Bumblespell said thoughtfully, "but I spilt a jar of dragon's whiskers, and I used my wand to magic them back."

"Excellent," Witch Willow-water said. "Now, you sit here and think about Thursday and Friday, and I'll fetch some Fizzy Wizzy Pie." She put her knitting down, and floated off into the house.

Wizard Bumblespell tried to think about Thursday. He found it hard to concentrate because the scarf kept changing colour, and the ball of wool seemed to have the hiccups.

"However does she manage to knit with wool like that?" he wondered. "Oh! Now it's gone sparkly!"

"Here you are." Witch Willow-water put a large slice of Fizzy Wizzy Pie down beside him. "So – what happened on Thursday?" She picked up her needles and went on knitting.

The Wizard tried very hard to think. "Thursday . . . Thursday . . . I know! I went to see Dragon Silverclaw, and we played Slithers and Sparkles, and I won every single game!"

"And did you use your wand?" Witch Willow-water asked.

Wizard Bumblespell went very pink. "Erm . . . it wasn't REALLY cheating . . ."

"What about Friday?" Witch Willow-water asked quickly.

"That was the day before yesterday, wasn't it?" Wizard Bumblespell said slowly.

Witch Willow-water dropped her knitting. "OH! On Friday I came to visit you! We sat in your kitchen, and drank Wizard's Best Brew, and then you lit the candles with your wand after I'd dropped up my knitting in the dark!"

Wizard Bumblespell was staring at the long woolly scarf as it tied itself into knots.

"Does your knitting always do that?" he asked.

Witch Willow-water frowned. "It's been VERY badly behaved these last two days. Maybe it got upset when I dropped it and you stepped on it."

"It tripped me up!" Wizard Bumblespell said indignantly. "I dropped my – AHHHHHHHH!"

He leapt up and grabbed at the knitting needles.

"What are you DOING?" screeched Witch Willow-water, and her eyes flashed. "You'll RUIN my knitting!"

"IT'S MY WAND! IT'S MY LOVELY LOVELY WAND!" Wizard Bumblespell waved something long, and sharp, and needle-like happily over his head. A shower of multicoloured sparks flew behind it.

"Why . . . SO IT IS!" Witch Willow-water stared. "I must have picked it up by mistake! But when?"

"In my kitchen!" Wizard Bumblespell was so happy that he danced round and round the table. "I found a knitting needle yesterday, but I never ever thought it was anything to do with losing my wand!"

"Well well well," Witch Willow-water said. "Who'd have believed it? No wonder my knitting was so twitchy! Oh – I'm really really sorry for the trouble I've caused you!"

She patted Wizard Bumblespell's arm. "I know! I'll knit this nice woolly scarf specially for you!"

Wizard Bumblespell looked at Witch Willow-water's half-made scarf. It was lying on the ground and not moving . . . but as he peered closer a shower of sparks flew up his nose and made him sneeze.

"Erm . . . it's very kind of you," he said, "but I think I'd rather not. I'd love another slice of Fizzy Wizzy Pie, though!"

There was a silence. Spotty Frog was fast asleep.

Wizard Gleek peered at Ruby. "Isn't Witch Willow-water your great granny, my dear?" he asked. "Aren't you a witchling?

"Yes." Ruby blushed. "But Spotty thinks I'm a human girl. I need him to help me find my stories, you see."

Wizard Gleek nodded. "So he's helping you because he's frightened you'll tell the children about our magic wood?"

Ruby hung her head.

"Well, little witchling," the wizard said, "I think you should tell Spotty the truth. He knows the witches in this wood are all good witches, so he'll be happy to help you. Is it for homework?"

Ruby shook her head fiercely. "I HATE witch school! I don't WANT to be a witch!"

Wizard Gleek looked surprised, but just then Spotty sat up. "Oh no!" he said. "I missed the end of the story!" He hopped off the rug, and bounced towards the door. "Thank you, Wizard Gleek!"

Wizard Gleek tucked a ball of wool into the story bag. "Ruby's got something to tell you, little frog – haven't you, Ruby?"

Ruby nodded.

As they walked away, Ruby began whispering in Spotty's ear. The wizard smiled, and went indoors.

Spotty was amazed when Ruby told him that she was a witchling.

"Are you sure?" he kept asking. "Are you sure?" until at last Ruby got cross.

"I should know!" she told him. "I mean, you know you're a frog, don't you?"

"I was a tadpole once," Spotty said. "Maybe you changed from a witchling into a girl?"

"NO I DIDN'T!" Ruby said. "I've ALWAYS been a witchling. Ever since I was born! And if you really want to know, I wish I wasn't. Now, I've said I was sorry, so can we PLEASE get on with collecting my stories?"

"OK," Spotty said. "We'll go and see the dwarves. This way!"

Big Toe and Grumblebeard were outside their houses,
together with Mrs Big Toe and Mrs Grumblebeard.
They were busy painting a sign that said,

BIG TOE AND GRUMBLEBEARD,
Best Diggers Ever!

When Mrs Big Toe saw Spotty she waved.
"Hello, Spotty!" she said. "Look! We're putting
up another sign! Who's your friend?"
"This is Ruby," Spotty said. "She's a wit – OW!"
Ruby trod heavily on his foot. "I'm Spotty's friend," she said.
"Yes," Spotty said as he rubbed his toes. "And we're collecting
stories, and I thought Big Toe or Grumblebeard
might have a story to tell her!"

Big Toe looked at Grumblebeard. Grumblebeard looked at Big Toe.
"I don't know any stories," said Big Toe.
"Nor me," said Grumblebeard.

Mrs Grumblebeard put down her paintbrush.
"Well, I do!" she said. "I'll tell you the story of how
Big Toe and Grumblebeard became friends!"

Big Toe and Grumblebeard

told by Mrs Grumblebeard

Dwarves are good at digging, and Big Toe was a wonderful digger. So was Grumblebeard. At the Digging Festival, Wise Old Owl judged them First Equal . . . but it didn't make them friends.

Big Toe dug a huge hole beside Wise Old Owl's tree. "I can dig much FASTER than Grumblebeard," he growled.

Grumblebeard dug an even bigger hole on the other side. "But I can dig much DEEPER than Big Toe," he muttered.

Wise Old Owl decided that something had to be done before his tree fell over. He flew down to the ground.

"I've got a challenge for you," he said. "Whichever of you wins will be Best Digger Ever, and NO MORE ARGUMENTS."

"Fine," said Big Toe, "because it'll be ME that wins."

"Fine by me too," said Grumblebeard, "because I'M going to win!"

"Good," said Wise Old Owl. "Now, I want you to work together."

Big Toe and Grumblebeard groaned loudly.

Wise Old Owl took no notice. "I want you to dig the biggest hole you've ever dug," he said. "You'll start when I hoot once, and you won't stop until I hoot three times."

Big Toe and Grumblebeard nodded.

"And you'll dig a LONG way from my tree," Wise Old Owl said firmly. "You'll dig right over there, beyond the stream."

Big Toe and Grumblebeard slung their spades over their shoulders, and marched over the bridge that crossed the stream. When they reached the other side they stuck their spades in the ground, and scowled at each other.

Wise Old Owl flapped his wings. "Ready . . . steady . . . HOOT!"

The dwarves began to dig. They dug and they dug, and the hole grew deeper and deeper. Wise Old Owl sat and dozed. Every so often he opened one eye to see how they were getting on.

Big Toe began to feel tired, but he didn't stop. Grumblebeard's back ached, but he didn't stop. Big Toe had blisters, but he kept on digging. Grumblebeard had a stitch, but he kept on digging.

Wise Old Owl opened both eyes as the moon came out. He could just see the top of Big Toe's hat, and the tips of Grumblebeard's ears.

"Hoot," he said to himself. "Not just yet . . . " and he flew away to find his dinner.

Big Toe and Grumblebeard went on digging.

By the time Wise Old Owl came back the sky was growing light. He peered down at the hole.

"Hoot," he said to himself, "that looks about right," and he hooted three times.

Grumblebeard and Big Toe threw down their spades.

"Well?" they demanded. "Which of us has won?"

62

Wise Old Owl smiled. "You'll discover that when you get out!" He stretched his wings, and with a "Hoot hoot!" he flew away.

Big Toe and Grumblebeard stared round. The hole was very deep indeed . . . far too deep to climb out of.

Grumblebeard had an idea. "If I climb on your back, Big Toe," he said, "I can reach the top!"

"WHAT?" Big Toe roared. "Do you think I'm stupid? No – I'LL climb on YOUR back!"

"That only shows you ARE stupid!" Grumblebeard bellowed. "I'm not letting you out first!"

"Then we'll have to stay here forever and EVER!" yelled Big Toe, and he sat down.

"See if I care!" bawled Grumblebeard, and he sat down too.

They sat without speaking for a long long time. At last Big Toe said, "That wasn't fair of Wise Old Owl."

"No," said Grumblebeard, "it wasn't."

There was another silence, then Grumblebeard said, "This must be the deepest hole anyone's ever dug."

"Yes," said Big Toe. "Even my uncle Elbow the Magnificent never dug a hole as big as this."

"My grandaddy Rufus Roaringbeard couldn't have done it," said Grumblebeard.

"It's a PRIZE-WINNING hole," said Big Toe.

Grumblebeard got to his feet. "It's SPECTACULAR!"

Big Toe coughed in an embarrassed kind of way.

"Ahem," he said. "I'm not saying that you dig BETTER than me, Grumblebeard old chap, but what I DO say is that you're not bad."

"You're not bad yourself," Grumblebeard said gruffly. He looked round the hole again. "This is something to show the others, you know."

"But we can't show ANYONE unless we get out," Big Toe said.

There was another silence.

"Ahem." Big Toe coughed louder. "Erm . . . if I DID let you climb on my back, Grumblebeard," he said, "would you help me out?"

Grumblebeard put his hand on his spade. "I swear by Iron and Wood," he said.

"That's good enough for me," Big Toe said, and he bent down. Grumblebeard climbed on his back, and with a great deal of puffing and pulling he finally managed to heave himself out of the hole.

"Wonderful whiskers!" he said as he looked down. "That's a DEEP hole, Big Toe! And WE did it!"

"YES!" said Big Toe's voice from below. "But Grumblebeard . . . it's filling up with water! My feet are wet . . . HELP!"

"Hang on, Big Toe!" Grumblebeard pulled off his thick leather belt and flung it over the edge of the hole. Big Toe grabbed the end, and Grumblebeard pulled . . . and pulled . . .

and pulled until at last Big Toe popped out of the hole like a cork coming out of a bottle.

From below came the sound of gurgling water.

"The stream must be leaking into our hole," Grumblebeard said sadly, but Big Toe's eyes were shining.

"It'll be a POND!" he said. "Grumblebeard – have you ever heard of dwarves digging a pond before?"

Grumblebeard shook his head. "Never!" He seized Big Toe's hand, and shook it up and down. "Big Toe! We've made HISTORY!" And they linked arms and marched off together . . . and not long afterwards a sign appeared by the tallest pine tree.

Do you need a pond?
A lake? A swimming pool?
Ask Big Toe and Grumblebeard.
Best diggers ever!

Wise Old Owl saw the sign, and hooted softly.

"Well done, dwarves," he said. "Well done!"

As Mrs Grumblebeard finished her story, Spotty looked puzzled.

"What happened to the hole?" he asked. "The big hole you dug?"

Big Toe smiled proudly. "Why – it's the pond where you live!"

Spotty's eyes opened wide. "My pond? YOU made my pond? Thank you VERY much!"

Mrs Big Toe patted Spotty on the head. "Dear little frog," she said. "Now, would you and your friend like a bowl of soup?"

Ruby and Spotty answered together.

"Yes, please!"

"No, thank you!"

"Are you sure, dear?" Mrs Big Toe looked encouragingly at Ruby. "You're a thin little thing."

Ruby frowned darkly. "We haven't got time."

Spotty, however, stood his ground. "Yes we have," he said. "It won't be dark for ages yet, and I'm HUNGRY!"

"That's right, m'dear," Mrs Big Toe said approvingly.

Ruby muttered crossly as she sat down, but when the soup appeared she had two helpings. "I didn't know I was so hungry," she said apologetically. Spotty was about to suggest that perhaps that was why she'd been so grumpy, but he thought better of it.

"Let's go and see the trolls now," he said. "Thank you, Mrs Big Toe. And thank you for the story!"

The dwarves waved as Spotty and Ruby went down the path.

"Funny little things," said Mrs Grumblebeard.

"Yes," said Big Toe, and he chuckled. "I popped a little silver trowel into that bag of theirs when they weren't looking. It'll remind them of our story!"

When Ruby and Spotty reached the
trolls' house there was no one to be seen.
"Oh NO!" Ruby said. "What'll we do?"
"Sit and wait," Spotty said. He hopped onto the
doorstep, and sat down. "You can tell me why you
pretended to be a human girl, if you like. And
why have you got to have your stories by tonight?"
Ruby shook her head as she sat down beside him.
"You're a frog. You wouldn't understand."
"I might," Spotty said. "I've helped you so far, haven't I?"
"I suppose so," Ruby said grudgingly. She scratched her ear.
"But it's all about fairies – "

"SPOTTY FROG!" Three trolls burst out of the bushes
and came leaping and bounding towards Ruby and Spotty.
"Hurrah! Have you come to play hide and seek with us?"
Spotty shook his head. "No," he said. "We've come for a story.
Ruby, these are my friends Lollibob, Mottle and Dada Tock."
"Hello hello hello!" sang Lollibob and Mottle, and they
shook Ruby's hand and patted her head and tickled
her toes until she was wriggling and giggling.

"A story?" Dada Tock asked. "We like stories, don't we, young trolls!"
"YES!" shouted Mottle and Lollibob. "Tell the mushroom story, Dada Tock!"
Dada Tock laughed. "You always want that story!"
"It's the BEST story," said Mottle, and he and Lollibob squeezed
onto the doorstep beside Ruby and Spotty. "It's about US!"

Mottle and Lollibob

told by Dada Tock

Once, when Mottle and Lollibob were little, their dada came home with a hat full of mushrooms.

"Oh my big hairy feet!" said their mama. "What beautiful mushrooms! We'll have half for our dinner, and we'll give the other half to Aunt Bulge."

"Can I take them to her?" Mottle asked.

"Me too!" said Lollibob.

"Well," Mama Troll said slowly, "it's a long walk. Do you remember the way?"

"YES!" said Mottle. "She lives under the rocks by the fairy ring!"

"Will you promise to go straight there?" asked Dada Troll. "And come straight back?"

"We promise," said Mottle.

"Straight there, and straight back," said Lollibob.

"Very well, then," Mama Troll said, and she put the mushrooms in a basket.

"Now, tell Aunt Bulge to enjoy the mushrooms, and say she can keep the basket as a present."

Mottle took the basket, and Lollibob waved goodbye. Then they walked away along the path.

"Straight there," Mottle said.

"And straight back," said Lollibob.

The two little trolls followed the path as it began to slope upwards, but then it began to twist in among the trees. Mottle stopped.

"Lollibob," he said, "the path's gone bendy!"

Lollibob nodded. "It's VERY bendy, Mottle."

"But we promised," Mottle said, "we said we'd go straight!"

Lollibob frowned. "But the path's not straight at all!"

"We'd better go through the trees," said Mottle.

"Yes," agreed Lollibob. "STRAIGHT through the trees. Then Mama and Dada will be pleased with us!"

So the two little trolls left the path, and tried as hard as they could to walk in a straight line. Sometimes they had to climb over fallen branches. Sometimes they had to crawl under bushes. Sometimes they had to wade through mud. It wasn't long before they were dirty and scratched, and their hair was full of leaves.

"I'm tired," Lollibob said.

"Me too," said Mottle. "It wasn't as hard as this when we went to see Aunt Bulge with Mama and Dada."

"Can we have a rest?" Lollibob asked.

"We must be nearly there," Mottle said. "Just over this rock – OH! FROLICKING FROGS!"

"FROLICKING FROGS!" echoed Lollibob.

They stood and stared at the stream rippling and twinkling in front of them.

"We'll have to wade through it," Mottle said.

"But we'll get wet!" said Lollibob. "I HATE getting wet!"

"We've got to go straight to Aunt Bulge's house," Mottle reminded him. "Come on!" And they splashed into the water.

"OOOH! AAAH! EEEEK!" gasped the little trolls, and they staggered out on the other side soaked to the skin.

"I'm COLD!" wailed Lollibob.

"Let's walk fast to get dry," Mottle said.

So on they went, and sometimes they had to creep through long grass. Sometimes they had to climb over rocks. Sometimes they had to wriggle under tree roots.

"I'm hungry," Lollibob said.

"Me too," said Mottle.

"Maybe we could have just one little mushroom?" Lollibob asked hopefully.

"Maybe just one," Mottle said. "After all, we're being VERY good. We're doing just what Mama and Dada said, and it's not at all easy going straight to Aunt Bulge's house!"

"One mushroom each?" asked Lollibob.

"One each," said Mottle.

They sat themselves down by the basket, and ate one mushroom each. Then they ate another, because Lollibob said just one mushroom would be lonely in his tummy. Then they ate a third. And another. And another.

"I suppose we'd better get going," Mottle said at last.

"Yes," said Lollibob. "Shall we have one last mushroom each to help us get walking?"

Mottle looked in the basket. "Oh," he said, "oh, whiffling whiskers! Look, Lollibob! They're all gone!"

The two little trolls stared anxiously at each other. "What shall we do?" asked Lollibob. "Shall we go home?"

Mottle shook his head. "No," he said. "We'll take Aunt Bulge the basket, and we'll fill it with something else."

Lollibob rubbed his nose. "Like what?"

Mottle looked round. "Leaves," he said. "We'll fill it full of leaves!"

It was easy to fill the basket with leaves, and they were soon on their way again.

"I feel better now," said Lollibob.

"Me too," said Mottle. "Straight ahead!" And they began to wriggle under tree roots and climb over rocks and creep through long grass until . . .

"Oh NO!" shouted Mottle.

"ANOTHER stream!" yelled Lollibob.

"But I've only just got dry," said Mottle as they waded into the water.

"Me too!" said Lollibob, and his teeth chattered.

"This stream's deeper!" Mottle moaned. "The basket's getting wet!"

"I'M wet AGAIN," said Lollibob, "and I don't like it!"

The two little trolls crawled out on the other side of the stream.

"Let's run," said Mottle.

"Do we have to run straight?" Lollibob asked.

"Yes," said Mottle, "but we must be really truly almost there, and Aunt Bulge'll look after us. She'll give us acorn tea and toadstool stew."

"YUM!" said Lollibob, and he began to run after Mottle. They splashed their way through mud. They threw themselves under bushes. They jumped over fallen branches, and then suddenly –

"DOUBLE-SIZED FROSTED FROGS!"

"WALLOPING WORMS!"

There, right in front of Mottle and Lollibob, was a path. And at the end of the path was a house . . .

and it was THEIR house, and Mama Troll and Dada Troll were outside waving.

Mama and Dada weren't cross. They laughed and laughed when they heard how Mottle and Lollibob had tried to go straight, and Mama rubbed them dry, and Dada made them acorn tea.

"We'll cook Aunt Bulge's mushrooms for supper," Dada said. "I'll find her some more tomorrow."

"But Dada – " Lollibob began, but Dada wasn't listening. He picked up the soaking wet basket and turned it upside down. Out fell lots of leaves . . . and seven shiny little fishes.

"FISH!" said Mama.

"My favourite!" said Dada, and that night they had a BIG fish supper.

"And the next time you go to Aunt Bulge's house," Dada said as he tucked Mottle and Lollibob up in bed, "DON'T LEAVE THE PATH!"

"Isn't it a good story?" Mottle asked.

"And all about us!" said Lollibob. "Now, let's play hide and seek!"

"We'll come and play tomorrow," Spotty said, "but just now we've got to go and collect the rest of Ruby's stories. She's got to fill up her bag before it's full moon."

"Have you?" Mottle asked. He snatched up Ruby's story bag and peered inside. "Why? What have you got in here? Is it magic? Are you a fairy?"

Ruby grabbed at the bag, but Mottle danced away with it. "Itty pitty fairy, can't catch me!" he sang. "Dancey prancey fairy, can't catch me!"

Spotty waited for Ruby to explode, but she didn't. She sank onto the doorstep and put her head in her hands. Shining silver teardrops slid between her fingers, and plopped onto the ground.

"Don't cry!" Mottle came running back. "Please don't cry!" He pulled a handful of mushrooms out of his pocket and pushed them into the story bag. "Here you are!"

"What is it, Ruby?" Spotty whispered. "What's the matter?"

"It doesn't matter," Ruby sniffed. She stood up, holding her bag very tightly.

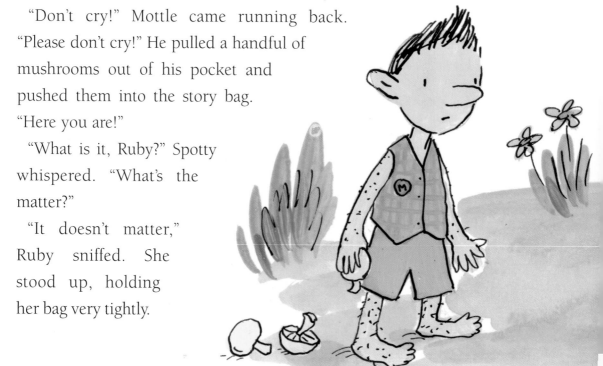

"Can we go and find the other stories now? Can we go and see . . . who was next?"

"Old Fairy Glimmerwing," Spotty said, "and little Fairy Peapod. They don't live far away."

"That's right," said Dada Tock. "You go down that path there." He handed Ruby a big hanky. "Are you all right now, little Ruby? I'm sorry Mottle made you cry."

Ruby blew her nose hard. "It's all right," she said. "He just made me think of something . . . something I want very much. Thank you for the story!"

Spotty and Ruby walked hand in hand to Old Fairy Glimmerwing's house
in silence. Witchlings were strange, Spotty thought. One minute they
were being bossy and horrid, and the next they were crying because
someone asked if they were a fairy. Still, at least she was nicer now.
Much nicer. Maybe, once they'd collected enough stories, Ruby
would be his friend and they could play together. But for now
he was happy to help her, and Old Fairy Glimmerwing's
house was right in front of them . . .

★ OLD ★
FAIRY
GLIMMERWING

and there she was, in her rocking chair with little Fairy Peapod on her knee.
Old Fairy Glimmerwing smiled. "If it isn't my dear little Spotty Frog!
You're just in time for Peapod's bedtime story. Make yourselves
comfortable, both of you, and I'll begin."

Spotty and Ruby looked at each other in amazement.
"Oh, THANK YOU!" Spotty said.
"Goo goo goo," said little Fairy Peapod,
and Old Fairy Glimmerwing began.

Fairy Mouldweed

told by Old Fairy Glimmerwing

Once, a long time ago, Fairy Mouldweed came visiting. No one had invited her, but she decided to come anyway. She arrived one morning, and she flew round and round until she saw what she was looking for – a neat little house in a tree.

"That's the place for me!" she said, and she dived down to ring the door bell. Owl answered, yawning.

"It's very early," he said. "I've only just gone to bed!"

Fairy Mouldweed didn't answer. She waved her wand, and Owl found himself tumbling out of his own front door. He grabbed at a twig, and pulled himself upright.

"Excuse ME, madam!" he began, but Fairy Mouldweed cackled loudly, and shut herself inside his house.

"This is MY house now," she shouted through the letterbox. "And I've put a spell on the doormat, so if you try to get in when I'm not here I'll turn you blue!"

Owl hooted angrily, and flew away to tell Wizard Gleek.

Wizard Gleek looked worried when Owl told him what had happened.

"I've heard about Fairy Mouldweed," he said. "She turns princes into slugs, and no princesses will kiss them better."

"But I want my house back!" Owl flapped his wings. "Couldn't you put a spell on her and magic her away?"

Wizard Gleek shook his head. "She's used to spells," he said. "What we have to do is make her decide for herself that she doesn't want to be here."

"Hoot!" said Owl. "You mean, make her uncomfortable? Keep her awake with hooting noises? That kind of thing?"

"That's the idea," said Wizard Gleek. "But she mustn't know who's doing it. She could make your feathers drop out with a whisk of her wand!"

Owl yawned. "I'll fly round and see who'll help," he said. "But would you mind if I had a doze first? I can't keep my eyes open."

Later that day Owl flew round the forest, and he could see that Fairy Mouldweed had been out and about. Two little pixies with pink feet were sobbing by the stream. Grumblebeard the dwarf was staring at huge purple caterpillars romping over his flowers. Big Giant Busybones was up a ladder rescuing the trolls who were clinging to his chimney pot, and bedraggled fairies were crawling out of the Lily Lake. Everyone agreed that Fairy Mouldweed had to go, but the pixies and the trolls and the fairies were frightened of what she might do if they tried to scare her away.

"It might make her WORSE!" whimpered a pixie.

"That's true," said Grumblebeard.

"I'd like to help," said Big Giant Busybones, "but she'll see me coming."

Owl flew back to Wizard Gleek with the bad news.

"Everybody's scared of her," he said. "What can we do?"

"I don't know," Wizard Gleek said gloomily.

"But you're a WIZARD!" Owl said. "You must be able to do SOMETHING!"

Wizard Gleek shuffled his feet. "I'm a GOOD wizard," he explained. "I can help people with my spells, but I can't do the sort of nasty things Fairy Mouldweed does. I can't magic up caterpillars, or turn pixies pink. She hates good spells. I love them!"

"Oh dear," Owl said. He pulled at a tail feather thoughtfully. "If she hates good spells, wouldn't a whole heap of them make her want to go away?"

Wizard Gleek stared at Owl.

"Owl," he said, "you're a GENIUS!" And he snatched up his wand. "QUICK!" he said. "Off to your house!"

"Let's go," said Owl, and within minutes they were outside Owl's front door.

"Right!" said Wizard Gleek. "Watch this!" and he waved his wand, and began to mutter.

Pink and red roses sprang from the ground and curled and twisted round the house and over the roof.

"Hoot!" whispered Owl in amazement.

"HOOT!" he gasped as drifts of butterflies fluttered among the flowers.

"HOOT HOOT HOOT!" Owl's eyes grew wide as his front door turned silver.

"OOOOOH!" he sighed. "It's – "

"DISGUSTING!" cackled an angry voice. "What EXACTLY is going on here?" And Fairy Mouldweed marched along the branch where Wizard Gleek was standing. The Wizard bowed.

"We wished to make you welcome, dear madam," he said.

"Welcome? Nobody makes me welcome!" Fairy Mouldweed barked. "You're supposed to hate me!"

Wizard Gleek bowed again, and an invisible hand offered Fairy Mouldweed a plate of pink sugary cakes.

"Be off with you!" Fairy Mouldweed waved her wand, but the plate dodged, and popped up on her other side. Another invisible hand offered her chocolate biscuits, and a third held out an ice-cream cone with a cherry on the top.

"Go AWAY!" shouted Fairy Mouldweed, and she waved her wand round and round . . . but the cakes and the biscuits and the ice-cream dipped and dived and spun around her.

Wizard Gleek bowed once more. A fountain of lemonade soared up into the air, sparkling and glittering, and a rainbow shimmered over Fairy Mouldweed's head.

"No no NO!" screeched Fairy Mouldweed, and she waved her wand so wildly that it slipped from her fingers . . . and Owl swooped down and caught it as it fell.

"GIVE THAT BACK!" Fairy Mouldweed was purple with rage, but Wizard Gleek took the wand, and tossed it into the air. With a puff of green smoke it disappeared.

Wizard Gleek folded his arms, and smiled.

"I think it's time you went home," he said. "Don't you?"

"Oh . . . BAH!" Fairy Mouldweed suddenly drooped. "I never did like this wood," she muttered. "Far too much yucky goodness . . . and those HORRIBLE roses . . . BAH!"

She stretched her wings, and flew off and away . . . and was never seen again.

"Well done, Owl," said Wizard Gleek.

"What did I do?" Owl asked, surprised.

"You that had the idea of Good Spells," said Wizard Gleek, and he touched Owl on the shoulder.

"Owl," he said, "from now on, you'll be called Wise Old Owl."

"HOOT!' said Owl.

As Old Fairy Glimmerwing finished her story, little Fairy Peapod sighed, and closed her eyes. The old fairy nodded at Spotty and Ruby.

"Fast asleep," she said. "Now, little frog, let's have a look at your friend!"

Ruby stepped back as Old Fairy Glimmerwing polished her spectacles, and Spotty saw that although the fairy was old and wrinkled and bent, her eyes were needle sharp.

"A little frog out and about with a witchling!" she said. "Mind out, little frog! You'd better run home to bed before the full moon rises! Even the littlest witchlings know a spell or two, you know!" And she picked up the sleeping baby and floated up from her chair and in through an open window.

Ruby looked after her, her eyes huge with longing. "Ooooh!" she said. "Don't you wish you could fly, Spotty?"

Spotty had never thought about flying at all. "Sometimes I wish I could hop higher," he said. "Or swim faster."

"I want to fly more than anything," Ruby said wistfully.

"Don't witches learn to fly on a broomstick?" Spotty asked.

Ruby turned away. "People can fall off broomsticks," she said shortly. "It's not the same at all."

Spotty didn't say anything more. Ruby obviously didn't want to talk about broomsticks. He hopped onto a fallen branch, and looked up at the evening sky. The sun was lying low on the hills, and it was beginning to grow dark.

"The pixies should be home by now," he said. "Shall we go and see?"

Ruby picked a handful of rose petals from the flowerbed by Old Fairy Glimmerwing's door, and dropped them into her bag.

"Lead the way, Spotty Frog," she said.

The younger pixies were playing a wild game of
catch-as-catch-can in and out of their houses and round
and round the rowan trees as Spotty and Ruby walked up the path.
Spotty pulled Ruby towards the tallest rowan where an older pixie was
sitting among the branches polishing the red berries to a glossy shine.
"I'm sorry to bother you," Spotty called up, "but might you
have a story for Ruby's story bag?"

"A story! A story! Tell us a story, Spangle!" The other pixies crowded
round as Spangle slid down from the tree. "We LOVE stories!"
And they flung themselves down on the grass to listen.
Spotty and Ruby sat down too, and Spangle laughed.
"I'll tell you a story," she said, and she tweaked Ruby's nose."
I'll tell you a story about Seed, Sparkle and Wink."

Seed, Sparkle and Wink

told by Spangle

Seed, Sparkle and Wink loved playing tricks. They tripped up the rabbits as they jumped out of their burrows. They posted pebbles through Mrs Mole's letterbox. They rang Big Toe's doorbell, and then ran away to hide. When Big Toe opened his door there was no one there . . . and that made him so cross his nose turned bright red. The pixies laughed and laughed.

Another time the pixies played a trick on Big Giant Busybones. Big Giant Busybones had a signpost that showed the way to his house, and they turned it round to face the other way.

"Nobody will find that old giant now!" Seed giggled, and it was true. When Wizard Gleek came to have a cup of tea with the giant he went the wrong way, and slid down the hill into the mud at the bottom. The pixies saw him walking home with his feet all dirty, and they laughed and laughed. Big

92

Giant Busybones thought the wizard didn't like him any more, and he was sad . . . but when he saw that someone had turned his signpost round, he was angry. He went marching out to see if he could find out who had played a trick on him . . . and the first person he saw was Big Toe.

"Have you been playing tricks on me?" he asked.

Big Toe frowned. "I certainly have NOT," he said. "That'll be those pixies! They do nothing but make trouble! I've just had to help Mrs Mole roll the pebbles out of her hallway, and there's mud on her new carpet!"

Big Giant Busybones pulled at his ear thoughtfully. "Seems to me," he said, "it's time someone taught them a lesson."

"That's right," agreed Big Toe. "But what can we do?"

"Well," Big Giant Busybones said slowly, "it seems to me they like playing tricks around houses. Why don't we play the same trick on them?"

"You mean, ring on their doorbell and run away?" asked Big Toe. "But I can't run fast enough."

"Nor me," said Big Giant Busybones. "But I could move their house."

Big Toe stared. "Are you really strong enough to move a house?" he asked.

Big Giant Busybones smiled. "Oh yes," he said.

"I know!" Big Toe said. "Why don't you move it tonight, while they're asleep? Then when they wake up they'll have a HUGE surprise!"

Big Giant Busybones nodded. "Good idea, Big Toe."

Late that evening, Big Giant Busybones knocked quietly on Big Toe's front door. Big Toe was ready, and he led the way through the trees and round the rocks until they reached a clump of blackberry bushes.

"There!" Big Toe said softly, and pointed.

It was a strange little house made of sticks tucked among the roots of the bushes. The curtains were drawn, and when Big Giant Busybones and Big Toe held their breath they could hear three tiny snores.

Big Giant Busybones bent down, and very very carefully picked up the little house.

"Where will you put it?" Big Toe whispered.

Big Giant Busybones just smiled, and began to stride away. Big Toe had to run to keep up with him.

"Here!" Big Giant Busybones had stopped in a little grassy glade where the stream came splashing over the rocks. There were bluebells and buttercups, and a tall beech tree spread its sheltering branches overhead. Big Giant Busybones gently tucked the little stick house under a tree root.

"This is a pretty place," Big Toe said, and he didn't sound pleased. "This won't teach them a lesson!"

Big Giant Busybones didn't answer. He sat himself down behind the beech tree to wait. Big Toe hesitated, and then sat down beside him.

The pixies woke as the sun rose. Seed flung open the curtains, looked out . . . and gasped.

"Sparkle! Wink!" he squeaked. "LOOK!"

Sparkle and Wink rushed to see. They stared and they stared, and then they tumbled downstairs and out of the front door.

"GALLOPING BULLFROGS!" said Seed as he looked at the bluebells.

"OH MY GREAT AUNT SLUGWIT!" said Sparkle as she saw the stream.

"BIG BUZZING MAYBUGS!" said Wink as he gazed up into the branches of the beech tree.

"It's BEAUTIFUL!" they all said together, and they sat themselves down to admire the view.

"How did it happen?" Sparkle asked.

"Someone's played a trick on us!" said Wink.

"But it's a GOOD trick," Seed said. "I LIKE it here . . ." and then he suddenly burst into tears.

"Whatever's the matter?" asked Wink.

"I know who moved us!" Seed sobbed. "It was Big Giant Busybones – nobody else would be strong enough . . . and we turned his signpost round!"

Sparkle began to cry too. "We were so MEAN!" she wailed.

Wink sniffed loudly. "We'll go and tell him we're sorry . . ."

Big Giant Busybones and Big Toe stepped out from their hiding place behind the beech tree. The giant was smiling. "That's what we wanted to hear," he said.

"But NO MORE TRICKS!" Big Toe said fiercely.

The pixies jumped to their feet. "No no NO!" they promised.

"Or else," Big Giant Busybones said, "your house might just move again . . . and next time it won't be among the buttercups and daisies!" And he winked at Big Toe, and they went off together to have breakfast at Big Toe's house . . . and when Big Giant Busybones got back to his own house he found the signpost was pointing the right way. And his house was clean from top to bottom . . . except for one shiny little pebble in the middle of the hallway.

"So you see," Spangle said, and she winked at Ruby, "we pixies don't always play bad tricks." She stood up and stretched. "Now, who's going to help me with the rest of the berries?"

There was a flurry of flying feet as the rest of the pixies skittered away as fast as they could go.

"Would you like us to come back and help you tomorrow?" Spotty asked.

Spangle shook her head. "You're a dear little frog to offer," she said, "but they'll come and help me later. Are you going home now you have your story?"

"We have to see Dragon Silverclaw first," Spotty said. He picked up Ruby's story bag and peered inside. "Our bag isn't quite full yet."

"Maybe these will help," said Spangle, and she dropped a bunch of rowan berries on top of the rose petals. The little bag gave a squeak, and Spotty and Ruby jumped.

"H'm," said Spangle. "A witch's bag! Do be careful, Spotty Frog. It's not long now until the full moon rises, and magic is in the air."

Ruby snatched up the bag and held it tightly to her chest. "We'll be very careful," she said. "Thank you for the story, but we must go now this minute!" And she ran off towards the path. Spotty paused to give Spangle one last wave, and then hopped after Ruby as fast as he could go.

By the time Ruby and Spotty puffed their way up the rocks and reached the entrance to Dragon Silverclaw's cave, the first star was twinkling in the sky. "Oh, please let the dragon be in!" Ruby said. "I only need two more stories, but it's getting so late . . . is he there, Spotty?"

Ruby had made Spotty run all the way, and he was out of breath. A wisp of smoke curled out of the cave, and he pointed to it as he puffed and panted.

"Hurrah!" Ruby took a step or two forward under the craggy rocks.

"Mr Dragon! Mr Dragon? Are you there?"

There was another puff of smoke, and Dragon Silverclaw came heaving out of the darkness. He was wearing a nightcap, and holding a book. "Shimmering scales," he rumbled, "I was just getting to the best bit of my story. What were you wanting? Are you carol singers? Clothes peg sellers? Postmen?"

"If you please," Ruby said politely, "we were wondering if you had a story for my story bag."

Dragon
Silverclaw

"Story?" Dragon Silverclaw said. "No problem at all.
How many would you like? I've a thousand thousand stories I could tell you.
A thousand thousand stories, to last a thousand thousand days."
Ruby looked so horrified that Spotty almost laughed. He hopped towards
the dragon, and spoke as respectfully as he could. "We would be most
grateful if you could tell us just one story, Your Silverness."
Dragon Silverclaw sighed. "If you're sure that's what you want."

He put his book down, and then looked brighter.
"But maybe you might want another when I've finished?"
"Erm . . . maybe," Spotty said.

The Princess and the Dragon

told by Dragon Silverclaw

Once there was a king, and a princess, and a dragon, and a castle. The king and the princess lived inside the castle, and the dragon lived outside.

The princess wasn't meant to play with the dragon, because the king was worried she might get burnt to a cinder by mistake, but right from when she was little she never took any notice of her father's orders. She climbed out of her window in the topmost tower, slid down the drainpipe, and ran across the grass to play tag with the dragon almost every day. On the days when it was too wet to play outdoors, the dragon flew up to keep her company. They played snap, and snakes and ladders, and they enjoyed themselves very much indeed. In fact, the princess was so happy playing with the dragon that she hardly ever played with her father, and he began to feel lonely.

"I think," he said to himself, "I shall order some knights to come and live here. Most castles have knights in armour about the place, and maybe one or two of them would like to help me cook, or do the washing-up." And he filled out the order form and posted it off. When he told the princess what he had done she just said, "Whatever," and ran off to find her dragon.

It was a sunny Tuesday when the knights arrived. They wore lots of shiny armour, and they clattered and clanged as they rode up to the castle. The princess and the dragon were outside, playing tag, and as soon as the knights saw the dragon they shouted, "AHA!"

The princess tried very hard to explain that the dragon was her friend, but the knights wouldn't listen. They caught him easily, because he didn't like to blow fire at them in case the princess got burnt to a cinder by mistake. He didn't flap his wings in case she got knocked over, and in no time at all they had him tied up and helpless. The princess burst into tears, but the knights just laughed, and poured buckets of water over the dragon's head so his fire went out.

"Can't have you burning your way out of those ropes!" they told him.

The princess ran to find her father.

"DAD!" yelled the princess, "DAD! Where ARE you?"

She found the king in the kitchen. He was looking hot and bothered, and he was stirring a huge panful of scrambled eggs. A little fat knight was telling him to hurry up.

"DAD!" The princess flung herself at her father. "They've tied up my dragon and they won't let him go!"

"Quite right too," growled the knight. "We're going to clip his wings and put him in a cage. He'll be a fantastic attraction for the visitors!"

"Visitors?" The king wiped his face with a tea towel. "What visitors?"

"Visitors to the castle, of course," said the knight. "You'll never be able to feed all of us lot unless you earn some money. People PAY to see dragons!" He opened a cupboard. "See? Nothing inside but a packet of mouldy biscuits."

He stopped to stare at the princess. "H'm. Pity you aren't prettier. It's a good thing we've got a genuine live dragon. Now – where are those eggs?" And he picked up the pan and marched off.

The king and the princess stared at each other.

"Dad!" whispered the princess, "we've got to get rid of them!"

The king nodded. "Yes," he whispered back, "but – "

Four big burly knights burst into the kitchen, followed by the little fat knight.

"'Scuse us," they said, and they picked up the king and the princess as if they weighed nothing at all. They bundled them up the stairs, and into the topmost tower.

"'Scuse us," they said again, "but we don't want you running off. We'll let you out when the visitors come."

"That's right," said the little fat knight. "With a ball and chain round your ankle so you can't escape!" And he locked them in.

The king put his head in his hands. "This is all my fault," he said. "It was me that invited them!"

"Don't worry, Dad," said the princess. "Just wait until it's dark and they're asleep . . ." and she gave him a hug.

It seemed a long time until all the knights were snoring loudly.

"Dad!" whispered the princess. "Wait here!" She picked up a pair of scissors, slipped out of the window, and slid down the drainpipe. She tiptoed across the grass, and the dragon opened his big golden eye, and winked at her.

The princess grinned, and pulled out her scissors. It took all her strength to cut the ropes, but at last the dragon was free. He bowed his head to the princess.

"Would you mind awfully if we rescued my dad?" she asked. "I know he's not been very friendly, but I can't leave him here."

The dragon nodded. The princess climbed onto his back, and with three flaps of his mighty wings they were hovering by the topmost tower. The king was leaning out, and the princess helped him struggle onto the dragon's back.

"Let's fly!" she said, and the dragon circled up in the air, and away.

When the fat little knight
woke up next morning and
found the dragon and the king and the
princess had gone, he stamped his feet in
fury.

"Everybody OUT!" he yelled, and the knights came
rolling out of the castle, rubbing their eyes and yawning.

"We're OFF!" said the little knight. "We'll never make any
money without a dragon . . . let's GO!"

"Fine by us," said the others. "The food was dreadful . . . did you try
those mouldy biscuits? YUCK!"

And they all marched away, and were never seen again.

As Dragon Silverclaw finished his story, Ruby began to clap. Spotty frowned at her, but she took no notice. "That was a WONDERFUL story!" she said. "Just the best!"

Dragon Silverclaw glowed with pleasure. "Thank you," he said. "Thank you, indeed. And now, for my next story – "

"AHEM!" Spotty coughed as loudly as he could. "Thank you, Your Silverness," he said, "but we haven't quite got time for another story . . . not now."

Dragon Silverclaw waved a claw at Ruby. "She loved my story! You'd like another, wouldn't you, my dear?"

Ruby suddenly realised what she had done. "It was the best story ever," she said, "but I'm really really sorry – I've got to do something very important before the full moon rises."

The old dragon sighed heavily, and picked up his book. "Always the same," he rumbled, "always the same. No one has time for a poor old dragon's stories. I'll be off and finish my chapter . . . " and he turned himself round and disappeared.

"I love stories!" Spotty called after him. "I'll be back to listen tomorrow! I PROMISE I will!"

There was a faint, but more cheerful, rumbling, and a shower of silver pebbles scattered around the story bag. One fell right in, and Ruby gave a gasp, and grabbed Spotty's arm.

"LOOK!" she hissed. "LOOK!"

Spotty stared. And stared. And stared.

The little story bag, now full and bulging, was growing two crooked little legs and a tail. It jumped to its feet, bobbed a bow at Ruby and Spotty, and began to scamper away.

"QUICK!" yelled Ruby. "CATCH IT!" She made a wild grab, but missed. Spotty leapt forward, but the bag was too quick. It ducked under Spotty's arm and headed down the rocks as fast as its bent little legs could carry it.

"COME BACK!" shrieked Ruby, but the story bag went on running. Ruby and Spotty scrambled after it, and Spotty was almost certain he heard it chuckle as it reached the path.

It was a mad chase. The full moon was lying low over the hills, but the forest was bathed in silvery light.

Ruby and Spotty ran and ran, but the story bag was always ahead of them, and always out of reach.

This way and that way and up and down it went, until Spotty and Ruby had no idea where they were in the forest.

When the story bag finally stopped and danced up and down in a doorway tucked between two silver birch trees Ruby fell on top of it without a thought as to where she might be.

"Welcome back, little Ruby," said a voice.

"And welcome to you too, Spotty Frog."

Ruby looked up, her eyes and mouth opening wide in surprise.

When she saw who it was she went pink, and then pale,

and stood as still as a little frozen statue.

"OH!" said Spotty. "Witch Willow-water!"

He tried to dust himself down, without much success.

"I'm so sorry . . . we were chasing Ruby's story bag!"

"You mean MY story bag," Witch Willow-water said.

Spotty looked at her in utter amazement. "YOUR bag?" he said.

Witch Willow-water smiled. "It's true, Spotty.
And I'm so glad to see that you've filled it up again, Ruby."
Ruby didn't answer. She handed the bag to Witch Willow-water,
and Spotty saw that she was trembling. Witch Willow-water
opened the story bag, and looked inside.
"Very good, Ruby!" she said. "These are wonderful stories . . .
much better than the ones you lost. But I think there's
room for just one more, don't you?"
Ruby still didn't answer, and Spotty looked from
her to Witch Willow-water in wonder.

Witch
Willow-water

"Sit yourself down, little frog," the witch said. "Ruby, you too . . .
I think it's time Spotty heard the last story of all."

The Little Witchling

told by Witch Willow-water

Once there was a witch, and she had a daughter. The daughter had a daughter, and this daughter had a daughter too – and of course we all know that witches only get to be witches by birth for three generations, so the last little daughter was only a witchling. Witchlings have to take tests and examinations before they can be proper witches, so this particular little witchling was sent to stay with her great grandmother to learn all the things she needed to know.

Unfortunately, the little witchling didn't want to be a witch. Not at all. She wanted to be a fairy, with sparkly wings and a magic wand, and she longed to be able to fly more than anything else in the world.

Spotty gave a little gasp, and looked at Ruby, but she was staring down at her fingers and wouldn't look back. Witch Willow-water nodded at Spotty, and went on with her story.

The witchling was afraid that her great grandmother would be very very angry if she knew that she dreamed of being a fairy. She never guessed that her great grandmother loved her very much, and just wanted her to be happy.

It was Ruby's turn to gasp. She gazed at Witch Willow-water, her eyes shining.

The witchling never told her great grandmother of her dreams. Instead, she made a plan. She decided she would run away, and look for the queen of the fairies. She knew the fairies came out to dance in the fairy ring in the centre of the forest whenever the moon was full, and she hoped that if she took the queen a wonderful present then she would be granted a wish . . . and then, at last, she could be a real fairy who could fly. The witchling tried and tried to think of a very special present, and at long last she had an idea. The great grandmother had a magic bag full of stories, and the witchling loved stories – surely that would be the most amazing and beautiful present for a fairy queen!

The witchling waited until her great grandmother was asleep one dark night. Very quietly she tiptoed into the workroom where the old witch kept her potions and magic spells, and she pulled the story bag out of the cupboard. Then away she ran . . . but what she didn't know was that stories have a life of their own.

Ruby gave a squeak of surprise, and Witch Willow-water put her arm round her shoulders and gave her a little hug.

Stories in a bag are very different from stories in a book. They need to be known and loved to stay where they are. If the little witchling had listened to her great grandmother telling her these stories before they would have stayed safely in the bag, but because she had never heard them they tiptoed out, and flew back to their cupboard . . . the old witch found them heaped on a shelf the very next morning.

The little witchling was very sad indeed. She thought the stories must have fallen out, but however hard she looked she couldn't find them . . . and how was she to give the fairy queen a present now? And she was much too scared to go home to her great grandmother, because she was very ashamed of what she had done. Instead, she went and hid by a pond, and spent a cold damp miserable night hiding in the reeds. Then, early the next morning, she heard a little frog singing as he hopped home. He was singing about fairies, and the poor little witchling suddenly had an idea. Maybe she could find new stories! Maybe the little frog would help her . . .

"Oh, have you seen the fairies oh, the fairies oh, the fairies oh."

Witch Willow-water put out her hand, and stroked Spotty's head. "And that's just what you did, little Spotty. And I thank you very much indeed. Ruby has a beautiful collection of stories, and I think the fairy queen would love them . . . but there's still a difficulty. Ruby, dearest, do you know what it is?"

Ruby looked up at her great grandmother and nodded sadly.

"Yes," she said. "The stories won't run away from me, because I know them, but they'll run away from the fairy queen . . . OH!" she suddenly sat bolt upright. "But what if I TOLD her the stories? Then she'd have them to keep for ever and ever and ever!"

Witch Willow-water laughed. "That's a beautiful idea, Ruby. But there's a much easier way, you know."

Ruby could hardly breathe. "IS there?" she whispered.

"What is it?" Spotty asked. "What is it?"

Witch Willow-water winked at Spotty, then turned to Ruby. "Wouldn't it be so much better if I gave you a wish instead?"

Ruby stared at Witch Willow-water as if she had never seen her before.

The witch nodded. "You worked hard to fetch those stories, and you've learnt a great deal. And nobody wants you to be a witch if you don't want to be – why, you'd get your spells wrong, and be almost as much of a nuisance as Fairy Mouldweed! Come here, my dear."

Ruby stepped towards her great grandmother, her eyes wide. Witch Willow-water took a shining silver star out of her pocket, and put it gently into Ruby's hand.

"Wish, my dear," she said. "Wish!"

And Ruby took the silver star, and closed her eyes . . . and opened them again. "No," she said, "no." She wiped a tear off her cheek, and knelt down beside Spotty. "This should be YOUR wish," she said, and she looked up at Witch Willow-water. "It was Spotty who found the stories, great grandmother. I was cross and grumpy, but he still helped me . . . it's Spotty who deserves it." She hung the silver star round Spotty's neck, and stood up, swallowing hard and rubbing her eyes.

"Well done, Ruby," said Witch Willow-water softly. "Well done indeed!"
She put her finger to her lips, and she blew Ruby a kiss . . .

TING-A-LING! TING-A-LING! TING-A-LING! TING-A-LING!

There Ruby stood, the sparkliest little fairy ever, with a pair of glittery wings and a tiny silver wand.

"Ooooooooooh!" gasped Spotty. "Ooooooooooooh!"

"THANK YOU!" gasped Ruby. "Oh, thank you – thank you – THANK YOU!" And she ran to Witch Willow-water and hugged her.

"And now," Witch Willow-water said, "you'd better hurry. The full moon is already high in the sky, and the fairy queen will be waiting to meet the newest fairy in her kingdom!"

And Witch Willow-water and Spotty watched and waved as Ruby flew into the air and circled happily before flying up into the moonlight.

"What sort of fairy will Ruby be?" Spotty asked curiously. "Will she be a tooth fairy? I've heard of those."

"Ruby will be a story fairy," Witch Willow-water said. "Every evening the fairy queen will send her to look for a little girl, or a little boy, or a gnome or a rabbit or even – " Witch Willow-water patted Spotty's head, " – a little frog, and she'll sit on their pillow and whisper a magical bedtime story . . . a wonderful story to send them to sleep with the most beautiful of dreams . . . "

"That's lovely," Spotty said, and he yawned a huge yawn. "Oh dear. It's been a very long day . . . I do wish I was in my bed."

TING-A-LING! TING-A-LING! TING-A-LING!

The next thing Spotty knew, he was waking up with the sunshine pouring on to his very own little lily pad . . . and there was a song inside his head just waiting to burst out.

Oh, do you know the fairy, oh the fairy, oh the fairy,
Oh do you know the fairy, who brings you magic dreams . . .
She brings you magic stories when you're drifting off to sleep
She brings you magic stories, the stories you can keep . . .
Oh, Spotty knows that fairy, and that fairy is his friend!

"And don't you go forgetting it, Frog!" said a voice in his ear,
but when Spotty looked round all he could see was a dazzle of sunlight . . .